Contents

Sam, the Wee Fat Dog, and the Saturday Bone

Sam is a dog, a wee fat dog, with short legs and a wobbly tummy. He lives with Jim in a bungalow in Scotland and likes to take life

very,

very

easy . . .

One morning Sam, the wee fat dog, was curled up in his basket fast asleep, dreaming about eating sausages and chasing rabbits.

Jim came into the kitchen and
pulled back the curtains. "Come
on, Sam, you're a lazy wee dog!
Don't you know what day it is?"

Sam's ears pricked up and he opened one eye. In two shakes he was on his paws. "It's Saturday!" he yelped. "You've got on your Saturday clothes!" He sniffed at Jim's old jeans. "Saturday! Saturday!"

"Oh, you're a daft wee dog!"
Jim laughed as Sam chased his
tail round and round in
excitement. "Look at you, Sam!
You can't wait to get your
Saturday bone."

"Bone! Bone!" At the magic
word, Sam was off again chasing
his tail like mad.

"All right then!" Jim clipped on Sam's lead and the two of them headed out of the bungalow, down the road, past the playground and into the shopping centre.

At the post office Sam did a happy roll-over. Mr McTavish said, "Sam's in good form, Jim."

Jim nodded. "Sam is always full of beans on Saturday."

"Here's your paper, Jim," said Mrs McCurdy the newsagent. "Where are you and Sam off to now?"

"The butcher's, Mrs McCurdy," replied Jim. "Sam can't wait to get his Saturday bone."

Sam headed for the door. "Come on, Jim!" he yelped.

With every step down the road Sam grew happier and happier. His tail wagged so much it nearly fell off his wee bahooky!

At last there it was, Mr McGregor the butcher's shop.

"Slurp and lick, bring it out quick!" Sam's mouth got ready to wrap round his Saturday bone.

Then he got a terrible fright.

Out came Mr McGregor with a great hairy dog on a lead. Even worse, the dog was carrying a bone bigger than the whole of Sam.

Mr McGregor tied the dog to one of the hooks in front of the window, where Sam always waited drooling and dribbling while Jim went in to get his bone.

"Oh, there you are, Jim," said Mr McGregor. ". . . and wee Sam." He bent down. "I've saved a nice bit of marrow-bone for you, Sam, the kind you like best."

Usually Sam jumped up and down when he saw Mr McGregor, but this time he didn't even notice the butcher. His eyes stared like two saucers as the big dog lay down and began scrunching.

"Maybe I'm having a daymare!" Sam closed his eyes, but the horrible hound was still there, as big as ever, when he opened them.

"Sam, come and say hello to Marco," Mr McGregor smiled.

"You can wait with him while
Jim gets his mince and your
bone. Marco, here's a wee pal for
you to play with."

Marco flashed a row of
gleaming teeth and went on
slurping.

"Pal!" gulped Sam. "I don't think that thing would be a pal for anything except maybe a mad elephant."

"Now don't be daft, Sam," Jim said and pulled Sam firmly towards the next hook.

"You usually like company. Marco's a nice dog." Jim patted the big dog's head and its tail flopped like a brush all over the place, throwing dust into poor wee Sam's eyes.

"Nice, my paw, Jim. He's scary! Don't leave me!" Sam whimpered. But Jim and the butcher were talking football and didn't hear. They went into the shop and there was just him and the horrible hound.

"I'd guzzle you up," Marco growled, "but I'm too busy right now. Just don't even look at this bone, that's all."

"Oh, no, I don't like bones very much, Marco . . . er . . . pal." Sam pulled as far away as he could.

Crunch, crunch, crunch! However hard he tried, Sam couldn't take his eyes off the big teeth making short work of the huge bone.

Sam almost burst with relief
when Jim came out carrying a
bulging bag with a lovely
butchery smell.

"Stay still, Sam," Jim pleaded
as he tried to untie the lead. Sam
had got himself twisted round
Jim's legs and yelped at him to
hurry up.

"Lucky I'm still chewing,"
Marco snarled as Jim finally got
Sam loose. "Otherwise I'd start
on your bone . . . or on you!"

"Help!" Sam stuck his tail
between his legs and ran as fast
as his wee paws would let him,
with Jim puffing to keep up.

Once he was in the garden
and the gate was safely shut, he
forgot all about Marco. "Oh,
slurp!" He grabbed his bone, ran
under his special 'bone' tree and
munched it to bits.

Sam had a lot to do all week.
He got the paper for Mrs
McGinty every morning,

kept cats away from the
garden,

lay on Jim's slippers

and did loads of other important things. Soon it was Saturday again.

The minute Jim came in Sam drooled, thinking about the bone waiting for him at Mr McGregor's.

"Mr McGregor's! Oh, no!" Suddenly he remembered Marco. Poor Sam!

"Howl and moan! I'll never get my bone," Sam whined sadly. "Let's not bother, Jim," he whimpered. "Bones are bad for me! I'm on a diet!"

Jim bent down and said firmly, "Now, Sam, what on earth's the matter? If this goes on, you're going to the vet's."

Sam slowly crawled out from under the table. Going to the vet was nearly as bad as Marco's teeth. "All right, Jim," he whined. "But it's your fault if that thing eats me up, bahooky and all!"

Sam dragged his paws all through the town. He stopped and sniffed at everything. But Jim kept walking and the butcher's shop got nearer and nearer.

Closer and closer they came. Sam's tail disappeared between his wee stubby legs and his tummy drooped so much it nearly bounced off the pavement.

Marco wasn't outside the shop. Sam began to feel hopeful. But, just as they reached the door, the same thing happened all over again. Out came Mr McGregor with the horrible hound.

Sam stuck his paws over his eyes and whined. "Munch and crunch, he'll have me for lunch."

"What are you lying there for, Sam?" Jim sounded quite cross. "Poor Marco can't get past to go home!"

"Home?" For a terrible minute Sam thought he was going to come and live with them. The shock made him open his eyes. To his surprise the big dog was climbing into a car.

"Thank you very much for taking care of Marco, Mr McGregor," called the driver. "Don't forget to bring us your goldfish when you go away for your holidays." With a wave and a toot, he drove away. Sam could see Marco chewing chunks off the seat.

He watched the car with the big dog disappear down the street and up the hill. He watched until it couldn't be seen at all. Then Sam went mad with joy!

"Sam, you're a daft wee dog right enough," Jim said as Sam lay on his back, waggled his paws and yelped with happiness.

Mr McGregor came out with a bone and Sam slobbered over him twice as much as usual. "Well, whatever the matter was with Sam, he's got over it now, Jim," laughed Mr McGregor.

"I suppose so." Jim shook his head. "But I can't for the life of me think what it could have been!"

"Oh, don't worry, Jim." Sam nosed the butcher's bag. "Just let me choose my own 'pals' in future! That horrible hound nearly put me off Saturday bones for good!"

Sam, the Wee Fat Dog, and the Boat Trip

Sam, the wee fat dog, knew
something was up the minute he
opened his eyes. Right in front of
his basket was a great big bag.
His nose twitched and in a wag
of a tail he was over at it sniffing
like mad.

"Oh, you've found the grub
already, have you?" Jim laughed
as he came in wearing a warm
jacket and a woolly hat. "Well,
just you wait a bit, Sam. This is
for the whole street, you know,
not just for us. We're off to sea!"

Sam wasn't sure what Jim
meant, but he gobbled up his
Popocops before the whole street
came and ate those *too*.

Mrs McGinty stuck her head round the door. "Oh, there you are, Jim! You and Sam had better get a move on, the coach is waiting outside. Here, I'll give you a hand with the bag."

"Thanks!" said Jim and snapped on Sam's lead. Then he and Mrs McGinty carried the grub-bag between them down the path.

"Come on," shouted the neighbours, "or we'll all miss the boat!"

They clambered on as fast as they could. Then, with a hoot and a toot, off the coach rattled through the town and towards the coast.

"I think it's a great idea to take a boat ride for our annual street trip, but do you think Sam will be scared?" said Mr McLuskie.

"Scared?" Sam's ears pricked up. "I'm never scared!" he thought and went on letting Mrs McGinty feed him Smarties.

Once they arrived at the harbour, the neighbours piled out and headed up the gangplank of the waiting boat.

"I'm not going up that thing!" Sam howled and dug in his paws. "What if my paws slip and I fall down the side, Jim?" He shivered until his wee fat tummy wobbled like a jelly.

"Oh, come on, Sam," Jim was as red as a beetroot. "Everybody is laughing at us." Finally he picked Sam up and puffed his way to join the others.

As soon as they were safely on board, Sam was as right as rain again and began chasing his tail in excitement.

"Keep Sam close by you, Jim," warned Mr Robertson the policeman, who lived two doors down from them. "Boats can be dangerous places for wee dogs."

"Don't worry, Mr Robertson," said Jim. "Sam won't wander away, he always stays near the grub."

"Quite right, Jim." Sam drooled. His tummy rumbled greedily as the neighbours carried the bags to a sheltered corner.

Wooooooooo. A warning whistle blew as the sailors pushed the boat off from the jetty.

"Oh, screech and howl, what a yowl!" Sam put his paws over his ears.

"Oh, isn't this lovely, Sam?"
said Jim as the mountains and
islands floated past.

"Lovely, my paw, where's that
grub?" Sam began nosing at the
bags.

"Look, wee Sam is hungry," Mrs McCurdy smiled. "And so am I. Open up, Jim, and we'll get started."

"Yum!" Sam was as happy as could be. Mrs McGinty had brought some apple cakes. Mr McWilliams dug out a box of round mints. Everybody had something to add to the pile of sausage rolls, pies and sandwiches

that Jim took out of his bag.

A big seagull swooped down and perched near Sam on a lifebelt.

"Keep away!" Sam growled. "This is *our* grub."

The seagull gave a rattle of its curved beak and flew onto the rails, watching with black beady eyes.

"Oh, this is the life," sighed Jim and handed a pie to Mrs McCurdy.

"So it is!" Sam began drooling as Jim picked up some sausage rolls.

"Here, Sam!" said Jim and threw one.

Then an awful thing happened.

Just as Sam was about to catch the roll, the seagull swooped down, snatched it and flew off.

"Come back with my grub!" Sam yelped.

Without a thought as to
where he was going, he chased
after the bird.

"Oh no!" shouted Jim and the
neighbours. "Stop, Sam, stop!"

But it was too late. Sam ran straight under the safety bar and fell overboard with a terrified howl.

"Help, Jim, help . . . !" Sam's cry was cut off with a great splash as he hit the water.

"Dog overboard!"

"Stop the ship!!"

"Go back!"

"Throw a lifebelt!"

Everybody ran about falling over each other trying to save Sam. In the confusion, nobody managed to do anything useful at all.

Down below, Sam sank like a stone and swallowed a bucketful of water.

"Going down, I'm going to drown!" he panicked. Then, all of a sudden, he began to float up again. In a jiffy he found himself on the surface, bobbing among the waves.

Sam had never been in deep water before. He didn't know that dogs can swim without having to be taught. His paws began to work like mad in a doggy-paddle, keeping him safe and sound, but a long way from the boat which was disappearing fast.

Poor wee Sam! He hadn't drowned, but it looked as if he would be spending the rest of his life in the water. Above his head, the seagull flew away laughing its feathers off.

Jim finally managed to get hold of the captain. "My poor wee dog is in the sea! You've got to go back."

"Oh, is that what all the noise was?" said the captain. "We'd better turn round then."

The boat turned slowly and, with a *Wooooooo*, headed back the way it had come.

The Captain looked out with a worried frown as they sploshed full speed ahead.

"If your dog is that wee, Mr McKinley, we might not be able to see him."

Jim and the neighbours stood at the rail, trying to spot Sam in the water. The sea was just so big. Would wee fat Sam be lost for ever?

"There he is!" shouted Mrs McGinty. "I can see his wee bahooky with his tail sticking up!"

Sure enough, there was Sam, still doggy-paddling like mad.

The gap between Sam and
the boat closed until they were
just next to him.

"How are we going to get
him out?" asked Mr Robertson,
peering into the sea. "It's a long
way down, Jim, and he can
hardly catch a rope or anything."

Everybody crowded the deck, scratching their heads and trying to work out how to rescue Sam.

"I can't swim for much longer," Sam yelped and got a mouthful of salt water again. "My paws are getting tired."

"Hold on, Sam, I'm coming!"

Jim threw off his jacket, grabbed a lifebelt and flung himself into the sea.

"Come on, Jim!" cheered the neighbours. "Good lad, you've nearly got him!"

"Yes!!" The crowd on the deck yelled and roared as Jim reached Sam and got hold of his collar.

Then it was all over. The sailors threw Jim a rope and pulled the pair of them on board with water dripping all over the deck.

"Three cheers for Jim! Three
cheers for Sam, the wee fat dog!"
shouted the neighbours.

Wrapped in blankets and eating pies and sausage rolls, Jim and Sam were the stars of the day. Everybody stopped to tell Jim how brave he was and to feed Sam biscuits. Sam wagged his tail so much, his bahooky was nearly as tired as his paws.

At home that night, happy, warm and dry, Sam curled up in his cosy basket. Jim bent down and tickled his ears. "What a wet adventure, Sam," Jim said, "but all's well that ends well."

"Right enough," Sam thought happily, "but next time we go away with the neighbours, Jim, I'm staying on dry land!"

THE END